Foreword

Why should we bother with books of fairy tales any more? After all, children can choose from a huge range of entertainments these days. You could be forgiven for thinking that computer games, multi-channel television and videos might seem far more glamorous to them than Mum or Dad reading dusty old stories about princesses and wicked witches and wolves in the woods.

The reason is, in fact, very simple. Children love fairy tales. They always have, and they always will. And that's because of the nature of the tales themselves.

At first glance, a story like *Little Red Riding Hood* might appear to have no connection whatsoever with the lives of modern children. But it does, and a very direct one, too. It's an object lesson about the perils of talking to strangers – in this case a large, nasty and very crafty wolf, who gobbles up Granny and then has Red Riding Hood herself for dessert.

Other fairy tales deal with vulnerable, small characters who face terrible threats to their lives or happiness, whether it's a giant who's after their blood, an evil enchantress casting spells, or that wolf again, huffing and puffing and generally doing damage to local architecture and the pig population. But the point is that there's usually a happy ending.

Children learn, therefore, that you *can* overcome even the toughest problems with bravery and thought and persistence. It helps that the stories are full of thrills and spills, plenty of jokes and terrific characters. They can do nothing but enrich the life of each child who encounters them, especially when they are presented in a way that does them justice.

And that's exactly what you'll find in Ladybird's *Stories for Bedtime*. Brian Morse has taken a new look at twenty of the best classic tales and brought them up to date with a fresh and exciting style that makes them great read-alouds. Enjoy them with your children – their magic will ensure that bedtimes are happy ever after!

Tony Bradman

Ladybird books are widely available, but in case of difficulty may be ordered by post or telephone from:
Ladybird Books – Cash Sales Department Littlegate Road Paignton Devon TQ3 3BE Telephone 0803 554761

A catalogue record for this book is available from the British Library

Published by Ladybird Books Ltd Loughborough Leicestershire UK
Ladybird Books Inc Auburn Maine 04210 USA

STORIES
for
BEDTIME

Chosen by TONY BRADMAN • Retold by BRIAN MORSE
Illustrated by PETER STEVENSON

Contents

The Three Little Pigs

Once three little pigs decided it was about time they left home and found their own place to live. No sooner said than done. That very morning they packed up their things, kissed their mother goodbye, and set off.

They walked till midday. Then they sat by the road and ate half their sandwiches. After a nap they set off again. By suppertime the first little pig felt too tired to go any further.

"But we haven't got anywhere yet!" his brother and sister said. "What are you going to do for a house?"

They were next to a field full of wheat that had just been cut. "I'll build a house out of straw," the little pig said. He closed his eyes and went straight to sleep.

When the first little pig woke, the sun was sinking fast and the air was growing cold. And what was that dark hairy shadow in the wood? Suddenly he wished he'd gone on with the others. But he set to work, gathered together some straw, and built his house.

8

At midnight there came a tapping at his door. "Little pig, little pig, let me come in," a voice said. The little pig's blood ran cold. Now he knew what the shadow had been—a wolf!

"You're not coming in here, not by the hair on my chinny-chin-chin," he said in his most grown-up voice.

"Then I'll huff and I'll puff and I'll blow your house in!" the wolf snarled. "And that'll be the end of you." And it was.

Next morning the other pigs came back. What did they find? A heap of straw and all their brother's belongings torn up and scattered across the field. They ran away as quickly as they could.

9

By midday the two little pigs were exhausted and stopped running. The second little pig began to think that they had reached a very nice spot. There was a pile of wood that a woodcutter had left, perfect for building a big strong house.

"Whatever happened to my brother can never happen to me," thought the second little pig. But that night, as the church clock struck twelve, there came a tapping at her door.

"Little pig, little pig, let me come in," a voice said softly. "I'm lonely and hungry. I want a bite to eat."

The little pig's heart gave a thump. Now she knew what had happened to her brother. "Wolf! You don't fool me! You're not coming in, not by the hair on my chinny-chin-chin!" she cried.

"Then I'll huff and I'll puff and I'll blow your house in!" the wolf snarled. "And that'll be the end of you." And it was.

Next morning the third little pig found the wooden house shattered to pieces and all his sister's possessions blowing in the wind. He began to run away but then he thought, "What did my sister and I pass down the road yesterday? A brick factory!" Back he went and bought enough bricks to build a house.

That night the wolf came prowling and tapping again. "I'm a friend of your brother and sister," he called. "Little pig, little pig, let me come in."

"Wolf, you're not coming in here, not by the hair on my chinny-chin-chin!" the third little pig shouted.

"Then I'll huff and I'll puff and I'll blow your house in!" the wolf snarled. He drew a deep breath and huffed and puffed with all his might. A wind that would have torn up whole woods hit the house, but the walls stood firm because they were built of bricks. The wolf huffed and puffed again and again, but only the doors and windows rattled. In a towering rage, the wolf leapt up onto the roof and began to climb down the chimney.

But the third little pig had thought of this. He quickly built a roaring fire in the grate and put a huge pot of water on to boil. Instead of landing in the fireplace, the wolf fell into the pot and was boiled up. His skin popped open and out jumped the little pig's brother and sister! The wolf had gobbled them whole!

How happy the three little pigs were to see each other again! Safe and sound, in the house built of bricks, they lived happily ever after.

Sleeping Beauty

Once a king and queen gave an enormous party to celebrate the birth of their daughter. After the feast the King told everyone how happy he was to be a father, for he and his wife had been waiting for years to have a child. Next he made everyone laugh with his story about learning to change nappies. Then it was time for the guests to give the baby princess their presents.

The last to come forward with their gifts were twelve fairies. "My gift to the princess is Happiness," the first fairy announced. The guests clapped and the King beamed all over his face.

"Mine is Beauty," said the second. "Mine Wisdom," said the third. And so they went on.

The twelfth fairy was about to give her gift when a clap of thunder shook the palace. The doors burst open and the guests cowered as an old woman shuffled in.

"The thirteenth fairy!" people gasped in horror.

The fairy's terrible voice hissed from the doorway, "Where's my invitation, King?"

"Someone must have forgotten to deliver it," the King mumbled. "Servants! Set another place! Quick!" Actually he hadn't invited her because he only had twelve golden plates for the fairies to eat from, so he'd decided to leave one out.

The fairy stood over the little princess's cradle. The baby gurgled and reached up her tiny hand. Suddenly the fairy cackled, "My gift is that on the princess's fifteenth birthday she will prick her finger on a spindle and die!"

With another clap of thunder the wicked fairy flew away. The palace doors banged shut. There was a terrible silence. Then the Queen began to cry.

The twelfth fairy stepped forward. "I have not given my present yet," she said softly. "I can't undo the evil spell, but I can change it. My gift will be that instead of dying, the princess will sleep for a hundred years."

Years passed and all went well. The baby grew into a healthy young girl, pretty and happy and clever. The King and Queen no longer thought about the evil spell. All the spindles in the land had long been destroyed. Surely the princess was safe.

But on the very day of her fifteenth birthday, the princess found a door she'd never noticed before. Behind it a staircase climbed into a tower. Up the princess went until she reached a door with a golden key. The princess entered a tiny room. An old lady sat at a wheel. "What are you doing?" the princess asked. The old lady smiled. "I'm spinning! Don't stand there staring, child. Try it yourself." She pushed the spindle towards the princess.

At that moment a terrible thing happened. The sharp spindle pricked the princess's finger and she sank to the floor. Down in the busy courtyard the hens stopped cackling. The princess's dog stopped chasing the cook's cat. In his study the King was writing his daughter's birthday card but the pen fell from his fingers. Even the kitchen fire stopped burning. The whole palace went to sleep.

Years slowly passed. The palace was forgotten. But a hundred years later a handsome young prince happened to ride by. He noticed a thorny hedge growing high in the distance. His servants laughed and told him an old story of an enchanted palace and a sleeping beauty. "But what if it's true?" the prince thought and rode towards the hedge.

At first he could see no way through. The hedge was far too thick and thorny for climbing. Then he drew his sword and began to hack his way in. The prince couldn't believe what he found on the far side. All round him animals and people stood and lay as still as statues. He walked through the palace. Not even a fly buzzed on the sunlit windows. No one moved. No one answered his questions.

Then he came to a half-open door at the base of a tower. Inside was a staircase. The prince thought he saw something gold glinting at the top. He bounded up the steps and a moment later was beside the princess. "Sleeping Beauty," he murmured to himself, leaning over her. He couldn't resist. He bent down and kissed her on the lips.

At once the princess opened her eyes. As she did so, the fire roared back into life down in the kitchen. In his study the King picked up the pen he'd dropped and finished writing his daughter's birthday card. The hens pecked for grain in the dust.

And in the room at the top of the tower, the princess saw the prince's face above her. For the first time in a hundred years she smiled. "Will you marry me?" the prince whispered. "Yes!" the princess said, and she kissed him back. When the King heard the good news, he ordered an *enormous* feast. The prince and princess were married and they lived happily ever after.

Rumpelstiltskin

Once a poor miller had a clever, beautiful daughter. One day he boasted to the King that his daughter could spin straw into gold. Of course this wasn't true, but the King believed him. So he locked the miller's daughter in a room full of straw and said that if she did not spin it all into gold by next morning, he would chop off her head.

The girl was sitting there weeping, not even trying to spin, when a voice said, "What will you give me if I do your job?" A strange little man was in the room.

"My necklace," said the girl. And the little man spun the straw into gold.

Next day the King locked the girl into an even bigger room. Again the little man appeared. This time the girl gave him a ring in return for his work.

The third day, the King promised to marry the girl if she did the trick one last time. He locked her into a room as big as a barn. When the little man appeared, the girl had nothing to give.

"In that case," he said, "when you are Queen your firstborn will be mine." Secretly the girl thought *Never!* All the same, she let the little man do his magic spinning.

The King was as good as his word and
they were married. In a year's time, the new
Queen had her first baby. How horrified she
was when the little man appeared. She offered him gold but no,
he would only have the baby. The Queen wept so hard that he
took pity on her. He said that if she could guess his name in three
nights, she could keep her baby.

The first night she went all through the alphabet: Aaron,
Bartholomew, Christian… None of her guesses was right.

The second night she tried funny-sounding names: Artitickle,
Danielslovel, Gumdroopy… But again she was wrong each time.

Then the Queen overheard a servant laughing about a strange
little man he'd seen in the forest dancing and chanting to himself,

"My name's not Elgin, Merlin, Finn or Larkin!
My secret name is Rumpelstiltskin!"

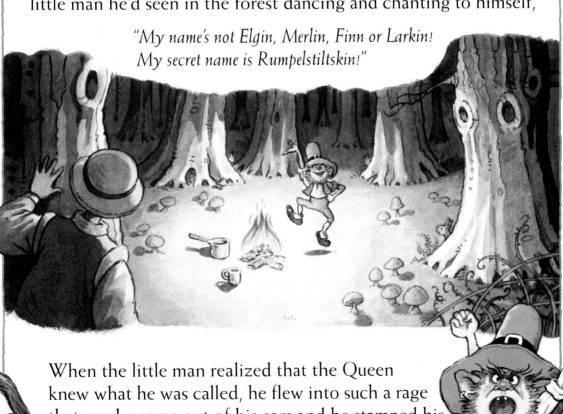

When the little man realized that the Queen
knew what he was called, he flew into such a rage
that smoke came out of his ears and he stamped his
foot through the floorboards. In his effort to pull
himself out, he split into two. And that was
the end of him!

Puss in Boots

Once there was a miller who had three sons. When he died, he left his mill to the eldest son and his donkey to the second son. The youngest got Puss. This made him most unhappy.

"What can you do with a cat?" he protested. "Cats don't even make a decent stew." Puss overheard that and spoke up quickly. "You'll find you haven't got such a bad bargain, Master. Just give me a bag and a pair of boots and you'll see what I can do for you."

Surprised, the boy did as the cat asked. Puss pulled on the boots and admired himself in the mirror. Then he took a lettuce and a juicy carrot from the pantry and marched off into the woods. There he opened the bag, arranged the lettuce and carrot inside, and hid nearby. Soon a tender young rabbit came along. He smelt the tasty vegetables and hopped inside the bag. In a second, Puss leapt up and tied the bag up tight.

Instead of taking the rabbit to his master, however, Puss headed for the palace, where he asked to see the King. Bowing low he said, "Your Majesty, I bring a present from my master, the Marquis." The King was delighted.

For three months Puss brought so many presents to the palace that the King began to look forward to seeing him. Then at last the day Puss had been waiting for arrived. "Don't ask any questions, Master," he said, "but go and bathe in the river this morning." Puss knew that the King would be driving nearby with the Princess, his daughter.

Later that morning, as the King's carriage drew near the river, Puss came rushing up all a-tremble. "Help! Help!" he gasped. "The Marquis, my master, is drowning!" Immediately the King sent a regiment of soldiers to the rescue.

But Puss had not finished. He told the King that while his master had been swimming, robbers had stolen his clothes. (In fact, Puss had hidden his master's rags in some bushes himself!) The King lost no time in sending for a suit of clothes for the Marquis. As you can imagine, Puss's master was feeling very bewildered at his sudden change of name, but he was clever enough to keep quiet.

As soon as the Marquis was decently dressed, the King invited him to ride in his carriage and meet his daughter. The Princess took one look at the Marquis, now dressed up to the nines, and fell in love with him.

Meanwhile Puss ran ahead. Soon he came to a field where some men were mowing grass. "Listen!" he cried. "The King is driving this way. When he asks you whose fields these are, you tell him they belong to my master, the Marquis. If you don't, I'll have you chopped into little pieces!"

Then Puss ran on a little further and came to a field where some men were cutting wheat. He repeated his instructions. Then on he ran again, and whenever he met anyone, he told them the same thing. At last he came to the Ogre's castle.

Slowly the King's carriage followed in Puss's tracks. Each time he came to a group of workers, the King asked them, "Whose are these fields, my good men?" Of course, he always got the same answer! The King was amazed at how much land the Marquis owned. (And so was Puss's master!)

Meanwhile Puss was very busy at the castle. "Ogre," he said, hiding a shudder at the Ogre's bad breath, "I've heard that you have the most amazing magical powers."

"Well, yes," said the Ogre modestly.

"For instance," Puss went on, "I've heard you can change yourself into a lion." In a flash the Ogre changed himself, and Puss fled to the top of a wardrobe, out of harm's way. When the Ogre had returned to normal, Puss came down. "Brilliant!" he said. "But changing into something small, like a mouse, must be impossible for a big fellow like you!"

"Impossible?" laughed the Ogre. "I can do anything!" In a flash he changed into a mouse. And… Puss ate him.

Seconds later the King arrived at the Ogre's castle. You can guess who owned the castle now! Puss met the carriage at the castle gates. "Come this way," he said. "A feast awaits you." (The Ogre had been going to invite a few friends round!)

By the end of the day, Puss's master, the Marquis, was engaged to the Princess. And by the end of the week, they were married. And Puss? Well, he lived to a ripe old age, using up every one of his nine lives, and he never needed to hunt a mouse again – but sometimes he did, just for the sheer fun of it!

The Twelve Dancing Princesses

There was once a handsome young man called Michael whose job was looking after the villagers' cows. All the local girls thought he was marvellous, but Michael didn't want to marry one of them. Come what may, he was determined to marry a princess.

Then one day a beautiful lady came to him in a dream. "Michael," she said, "go to the castle of Belœil. Find your princess there."

When he told the villagers, they jeered, "Cowherds don't marry princesses!" But Michael believed his dream. Next morning he set off to seek his fortune.

As it happened, he couldn't have gone to the castle at a better time, for something strange was happening there. The King's twelve beautiful daughters all slept in the same room, which was locked and bolted each night at bedtime. Yet in the morning the Princesses were as tired as if they'd been up all night. Even more mysteriously, the soles of their dancing shoes were worn out each morning.

The Princesses said, "All we do is sleep!"

But the King didn't believe that. He announced that if any prince discovered their secret, he could choose one of the Princesses for his bride. Prince after prince had been locked in with the Princesses. None of them had ever been seen again.

When he reached the castle, Michael got a job as a gardener. One of his duties was to give the Princesses a bouquet of flowers each morning. As soon as Michael set eyes on the youngest Princess, he knew that she was the one for him. He could tell she liked the look of him too, even though he was only a gardener.

22

That night he had another dream. The lady told him to plant two trees. When they grew they would grant him any wish.

Strangely enough, two young trees were by his side when he woke. He planted them and as soon as they'd grown, he said, "Make me invisible!"

His wish was granted. That night the invisible Michael hid in the Princesses' room. As soon as the door had been locked, the Princesses put on their party clothes.

Then the eldest clapped her hands three times and a trap door opened. Down a hidden staircase the Princesses went, with Michael following, but carelessly he stepped on the hem of the youngest Princess's dress.

Frightened, she called, "Someone is holding my dress!"

"Silly!" her eldest sister called back. "It caught on a nail."

At the bottom of the staircase was a grove of beautiful trees with silver-spangled leaves. Beyond that was another with gold-spangled leaves, then another where the leaves were studded with diamonds.

At last they reached a lake where twelve boats waited. On the far side was a castle. Michael climbed into the youngest Princess's boat.

"Hurry! We're getting left behind," she complained to the Prince who was rowing it. (He was one of the Princes who'd so mysteriously disappeared.)

"It seems heavier tonight," the poor Prince said, rowing his hardest.

In the castle, a ball was in full swing. All night Michael watched the youngest Princess dancing. How lovely she was! How beautifully she danced!

At three in the morning, the Princesses' dancing shoes were worn out. Back across the lake they were rowed. As they passed through the grove of silver-spangled leaves, Michael snapped off a spray of them.

In the morning Michael pushed the spray into the youngest Princess's bouquet. She saw it but said nothing.

The second night Michael followed again. Next morning the youngest Princess saw a sprig of gold-spangled leaves in her bouquet.

"You know our secret!" she said to Michael. She offered him gold not to tell the King. Michael refused it. In desperation the youngest Princess told her sisters.

"Throw him in a dungeon!" they said. But the youngest Princess said, "No!"

"Then let your gardener come with us," the sisters said. "We'll drug him like the others."

That night Michael had no need to wish himself invisible. Instead he wished for a magnificent suit of clothes so that he could look like a prince. He went with the Princesses to the ball and danced all night. Then, while they were resting, the eldest brought him a glass of drugged wine.

Now, Michael had heard all about this plot when he was invisible, but he could not bear to be parted from the youngest Princess, so he put the glass to his lips. He was about to drink, when she knocked it out of his hand.

"I don't want you to be like the others!" she cried. "I want us to live in the everyday world, even if it *does* mean I become a gardener's wife!" Bursting into tears, she threw herself into Michael's arms.

All at once, it was as though a spell had been broken. The real Princes suddenly remembered who they were and immediately asked the other Princesses to marry them. The Princesses had been enchanted by the magical world they had visited so often, but now they were overjoyed to find real happiness at last.

But the story ends even more happily than that, for when the King heard how Michael had broken the spell, he made him a prince too. So the youngest Princess didn't have to marry a gardener after all!

The Three Billy Goats Gruff

Once there were three brothers, the three billy goats Gruff, who lived in a land of high mountains and deep ravines. One day the brothers were out chewing thorns and thistles on a stony hillside and not enjoying their food very much.

The smallest goat, whose mouth was much softer than his brothers', stopped for a rest. He looked over to the hillside opposite and what did he see? The most luscious green grass a billy goat had ever set eyes on!

"Brothers!" he bleated. "Follow me!" Down the bank he bounded. There was a stream at the bottom with a bridge over it, and the youngest billy goat began to run across the bridge.

"Stop!" his brothers shouted, but far too late. In the ravine under the bridge lived a troll with the sharpest teeth and ugliest eyes in the whole wide world.

"Stop! Stop!" the brothers called, but the troll was already poking his head over the edge of the bridge.

"Who's that trip-trapping over my bridge?" the troll screamed.

When he saw the troll, the smallest billy goat trembled from the tip of his wet nose to the end of his feathery tail.

"I'm little billy goat Gruff," he bleated. "I'm only crossing your bridge to get to the young green grass on the other side."

The troll licked his lips with his enormous rough tongue. "Oh no, you're not!" he shouted. He began to wriggle his way up onto the bridge. "I'm going to gobble you up."

"But my brother's coming after me!" the little billy goat bleated. "And he's much *much* fatter than me."

The greedy troll immediately dropped out of sight and the smallest billy goat ran on over the bridge to the other side.

The two older brothers put their heads together to decide what to do, and a minute later the middle-sized billy goat Gruff rather reluctantly came down the hillside. *Trip, trap, trip, trap,* went his hooves on the bridge. Immediately the troll raised his head above the edge.

"Who's that trip-trapping over my bridge?" he screamed.

"I'm middle-sized billy goat Gruff," the goat bleated, "and I'm going across to join my younger brother."

"Oh no, you're not!" the troll shouted. He began to clamber onto the bridge. "You look fat and juicy. I'm going to gobble you up."

"But my other brother's coming after me!" bleated the middle-sized goat, at the same time trying to make himself look as small as possible. "He's much, much, *much* fatter than me."

The greedy troll immediately dropped out of sight and, with a sigh of relief, the middle-sized billy goat ran over to the other side of the bridge.

After a minute the largest billy goat Gruff started trip-trapping over the bridge too. *Trip, trap, trip, trap, trip, trap,* went his hooves on the bridge.

The troll could hardly contain his excitement at the meal he was going to have. "Who's that trip-trapping over my bridge?" he screamed.

"I'm big billy goat Gruff," the third brother bleated, "and I'm going across to the other side to join my brothers in the lovely green grass."

"Oh no, you're not!" the troll shouted. "No, no, no!" With his long hairy arms he pulled himself straight up onto the bridge. "I'm going to gobble you up! That's what's going to happen!"

The moment the troll's feet landed on the bridge, he realized he'd made a big mistake. Big billy goat Gruff was massive. His horns were longer and sharper than all the troll's teeth put together.

As the goat put his head down and charged, the troll screamed, "No, no, no!" He tried to dive back under the bridge, but far too late. The goat's horns tossed him into the stream and the raging water carried him away. No one ever found out what happened to him and no one cared!

The big billy goat Gruff trip-trapped proudly over the rest of the bridge and joined his two brothers. Perhaps he had a few words to say to the smallest billy goat for putting them all in danger, but certainly the Gruffs enjoyed the young green grass and lived happily ever after.

Hansel and Gretel

There were once two children called Hansel and Gretel whose mother had died when they were very small. After some years their father, who was a woodcutter, married again. His new wife came from a much better-off family. She hated living in a poor cottage at the edge of the forest and having hardly anything to eat. And she particularly hated her two stepchildren.

One bitter winter evening, when they were in bed, Hansel and Gretel overheard their stepmother say, "We've hardly any food left. If we don't get rid of the children, we'll *all* starve to death."

The father let out a cry. "It's no use arguing," his wife said. "My mind's made up. Tomorrow we'll lose them in the forest."

"Don't worry," Hansel comforted his sister. "We'll find our way home." Later that night he crept outside and filled his pockets with pebbles.

In the morning the family set off. As they walked, Hansel secretly dropped the pebbles one by one behind him to make a trail. At midday the parents lit a fire for the children and promised to be back soon. They disappeared into the forest but, of course, they never returned.

Shivering with fear, while wolves howled all around them, Hansel and Gretel stayed by the fire until the moon came out and lit the trail of pebbles. Quickly they followed it home.

Their father was overjoyed to see them. Their stepmother pretended she was too but her mind hadn't changed. Three days later she decided to try again. That night she locked the door. She wasn't having Hansel collect pebbles this time. But Hansel was clever. When they set off in the morning, he left a trail of crumbs from the crust meant for his dinner.

At midday the parents left the children as before. When they did not return, Hansel and Gretel waited patiently for the moon to light their way home. But this time the trail had gone. Birds had eaten the crumbs!

Now the children really were lost. They wandered through the forest, starving and frightened, for three days and nights. On the third day they caught sight of a snow-white bird in the branches of a tree. The bird sang to them and the children forgot their hunger and ran after it. It led them to an extraordinary house, built with walls of bread, a roof of cake and windows of sparkling sugar.

At once the children forgot their troubles and ran towards the house. Hansel was about to eat a slice of roof and Gretel a piece of window when a voice called from inside, "Who's nibbling my house?" Out of the door came the sweetest-looking old lady. "You poor dears," she said. "Come inside." Soon the children were eating the largest meal they'd had in their lives. That night they slept on feather beds.

But in the morning everything changed. The old lady was a witch who'd built her house of bread and cake to trap unwary children. She dragged Hansel out of bed by his hair and locked him in a shed. Then she pushed Gretel downstairs into the kitchen.

"Your brother's nothing but skin and bone!" she screamed. "Cook for him! Fatten him up! When he's plump enough he'll make me a lovely meal! But eat nothing yourself! It's all for him." Gretel cried and cried but she had to do as the witch said.

Luckily Hansel still had his wits about him. He decided to fool the witch, whose eyesight was not very good. Every morning she came to feel his finger to see if he was fattening up. Instead of his finger, Hansel pushed a chicken bone through the bars of the window for the witch to feel. "No good! Not fat enough!" she shouted. Back into the kitchen she went and forced Gretel to make bigger and bigger meals.

This went on for a month, until at last the witch's patience ran out. "Fat or thin, today I'm baking Hansel pie!" she screamed at Gretel. "Check if the pastry is baking properly." But Gretel had her wits about her too. She knew the witch meant to push her into the oven.

"I can't get my head in! I can't see the pastry!" she wailed. With a blow the witch knocked Gretel aside and pushed her own head into the oven. Gretel summoned all her strength, gave the evil old lady a huge push, and slammed the oven door after her.

Hansel was free, yet the children were still lost. They set off again through the forest. When they reached a river, a duck carried first Hansel and then Gretel across. Suddenly the children recognized where they were. They ran home as fast as they could.

How happy their father was to see them! He cried with joy as he told them that their cruel stepmother had gone back to her family soon after they'd been lost in the forest. He told them how heartbroken he'd been when he realized what he had done.

And there was another surprise in store for him. Hansel emptied out his pockets and Gretel her apron. They were full of gold and diamonds they had found in the witch's house. Now all the family's worries were over and from then on they all lived together in sheer happiness.

The Fisherman and His Wife

There were once an old man and an old woman who lived in a pigsty. They were so untidy and messy that the pigs had moved out long ago! The old man's hobby was fishing. One day he was sitting on the seashore fishing away to his heart's content when his line was nearly torn from his hands.

"Wow!" he thought. "This is going to be a biggun! I may even have caught a shark or a whale!" So he hauled away until the fish he'd caught (in fact it was a great big flounder) came flip-flapping onto the beach.

The old man had taken out the hook and was wondering how he was going to carry the fish home when the flounder said, "Now look here, old fellow, don't eat me. I wouldn't taste right. I'm not really a fish but an enchanted prince."

The old man was startled out of his wits. "Don't worry," he said. "I don't want anything to do with a talking fish." And he hastily shoved the fish back in the water and watched him swim away.

"Guess what!" said the old man to his wife when he got back home. He told her the whole story.

"You old idiot!" said his wife. "You mean you caught an enchanted prince and you didn't even ask for a wish?"

"The flounder didn't say anything about a wish," the old man said doubtfully.

"He might not have," his wife replied, "but he *should* have. Go back and tell him! Now! Off you go!" She pushed him out of the pigsty with her broom.

The old man was rather nervous but all the same he stood on the seashore and called,

> *"Prince Flounder, enchanted fish,*
> *My wife Ethel wants me to get our wish."*

At first nothing happened. Then the water swirled about a bit and the flounder stuck his head out of the water.

"My wife wants to live in a bungalow," the old man shouted.

"Go home. Your wish has been granted," the flounder said, and with a grunt he disappeared beneath the waves.

When he got home, the old man found that instead of a pigsty he and his wife were living in a bungalow. It had a bathroom and toilet, a proper kitchen, a fire in the living room and a neat little garden. His wife was purring with happiness.

All went well for a couple of weeks until one morning the old woman woke her husband with an elbow in the ribs. "A bungalow isn't good enough for the likes of me," she said. "Go back and tell that fish of yours I want a big country house. Go on, out of bed this instant! And," she shouted after him, "I want a butler too. And servants!"

The old man stood on the seashore and very nervously called,

*"Prince Flounder, enchanted fish,
My wife Ethel has another wish."*

The water frothed about a good deal this time but eventually the flounder appeared. "Go home," the fish said. "I know all about your wife's wish. It has been granted." And so it had.

And for a couple of months all went well. But one morning the old man was woken by the butler with a message from his wife.

"A palace?" the old man said. "She wants a palace! What else? To be King as well?" He was joking really.

"Yes, sir, I rather think that was the idea," the butler said politely.

For the third time the old man went back to the seashore. This time the waves beat so high on the beach that the old man was drenched before the flounder appeared, but even so the wife's wish was granted.

36

The old woman loved being King, and all went well for a couple of years until one morning a regiment of soldiers drew up beneath the old man's window.

"Your wife, the King, orders you on pain of death to go back to the fish," the general bellowed. "She wants to be made Ruler of the World. She wants to be able to turn the sun and moon on and off when she likes." The general stamped his feet and saluted.

This time a storm was raging on the seashore as the old man delivered his message. The waves were as high as mountains. At last the flounder appeared.

"Well, old man, what does your wife want now?" the fish demanded. Full of fear and trembling, the old man told him.

"Go home," the flounder commanded. "She's back in the pigsty already."

And you know, she and the old man are living there still.

Rapunzel

Once a man and his wife longed and longed for a child of their own. Then at last the wife discovered that she was expecting a baby.

One day the wife was standing at a high window, gazing down into a neighbouring garden full of beautiful flowers and vegetables, when her eye fell on a bed of special lettuces. Immediately it was as if a spell had been put on her. She could think of nothing else.

"I have to have some of that lettuce or I'll die," she told herself. She stopped eating and began to waste away.

Eventually her husband grew so worried that, one evening, he climbed over the wall into the neighbouring garden and picked a handful of lettuce leaves. This was a very brave thing to do, as the garden belonged to a powerful witch.

His wife ate the lettuce greedily, but the handful wasn't enough. Her husband had to go back next evening. This time the witch was lying in wait for him.

"How dare you sneak in and steal from me!" she screeched. "You will pay for this!"

The husband begged to be forgiven. He explained how badly his wife needed the lettuce.

"In that case," the witch said more softly, "take as much as she wants. But when the baby is born, you must give it to me." The husband was so terrified that he agreed.

A few weeks later the baby arrived. That same day, the witch came to take away the newborn child. She called her Rapunzel because that was the name of the kind of lettuce that the mother had wanted so badly.

The witch cared for the little girl well. When Rapunzel was twelve years old, she was the most beautiful child in the world. Then the witch took her to a high tower in the middle of a forest. This tower had no stair, just a tiny window at the top.

When the witch wanted to visit, she called, "Rapunzel! Rapunzel! Let down your golden hair!" and Rapunzel would hold her long, braided hair over the windowsill for the witch to climb.

This went on for several years, until one day a king's son came hunting in the forest. From far away he heard the sound of a lovely voice singing. He rode here and there among the trees until he came to the tower but he could see no way up it.

Haunted by the voice, he came back again and again until one day he saw the witch and watched how she got into the tower. Next day as it was growing dark, he called out softly, "Rapunzel! Rapunzel! Let down your golden hair!" A minute later he was with the girl.

At first Rapunzel was frightened, for she had never had any visitors except the witch, but the Prince gently explained how he'd heard her singing and fallen in love with her voice. When she felt less afraid, he asked her to marry him, and blushing, Rapunzel agreed.

But how was Rapunzel to escape? The clever girl had a brilliant idea. The Prince must bring skeins of silk each time he visited. Rapunzel could make them into her own ladder.

All went well and the witch noticed nothing until one day, without thinking, Rapunzel said, "Mother, why is it easier for the Prince to climb up my hair than you?" Then the truth was out.

"You wicked girl! How you have deceived me! I meant to keep you free of the world's evil," the witch raved. She caught hold of Rapunzel and cut off her hair, then sent her to live in a faraway desert place.

That same night, the witch lay in wait for the Prince. When he called out, "Rapunzel! Rapunzel! Let down your golden hair!" she let down the girl's chopped-off hair and hauled him up. The Prince was at her mercy.

"The cat has taken the bird," the witch hissed. "She'll sing no more for you."

In despair the Prince threw himself from the window. He wasn't killed, but the brambles below scratched his eyes. For several years he wandered blindly through the forest, weeping for his lost Rapunzel and living on roots and berries.

Then one day he reached the desert place where Rapunzel was living. Far off he heard a sweet voice singing.

"Rapunzel! Rapunzel!" he called. Rapunzel cried with joy at seeing her Prince again, and two of her tears fell on his eyes. A miracle happened, and the Prince could see again.

The happy couple travelled back to the Prince's kingdom, where they were received with great joy and lived happily ever after.

The Gingerbread Boy

Once upon a time an old lady thought how nice it would be to have a little boy about the house again.

"A boy?" her husband said. "We're too old for that sort of caper!" But he saw that she'd made up her mind so he said, "Why not bake a gingerbread boy?"

"What a marvellous idea!" the old lady exclaimed. She mixed up the ingredients, rolled out the dough, then cut out the shape of a gingerbread boy.

She gave him currants for eyes, a smiley mouth, a waistcoat and a hat. She even put buttons down the front of his waistcoat and go faster stripes on his shoes! Then she popped him into the oven to bake.

When the timer on the cooker rang, the old lady opened the oven door. But the gingerbread boy didn't lie still on the baking tray. He leapt straight out onto the floor and ran away through the kitchen door. The astonished old man and lady called to him to come back, but the gingerbread boy felt very grown-up and he shouted,

"Run, run, as fast as you can,
You won't catch me, I'm the gingerbread man!"

Down the road he ran, through a stile and into a field where a cow was chewing grass.

"Hey!" the cow mooed. "Stop and give me a bite to eat!"

The gingerbread boy thought that was really funny. "I've run away from a man and a woman, and now I'll run away from you!" Putting on speed, he shouted,

> "Run, run, as fast as you can,
> You won't catch me, I'm the gingerbread man!"

The cow ran after him in a rather wobbly sort of way, but it was no use. She couldn't catch him.

Next the gingerbread boy came to a horse. "Hey!" the horse neighed. "I'm hungry. Give me a nibble!"

But the gingerbread boy just laughed. "I've run away from a man and a woman and a cow, and now I'll run away from you!" He ran even faster, shouting,

> "Run, run, as fast as you can,
> You won't catch me, I'm the gingerbread man!"

The horse galloped after him but he couldn't catch him.

Next the gingerbread boy met some joggers panting along a path. "Hey! Stop!" they called. "We haven't had our breakfast yet!"

But the gingerbread boy just skipped past them. "I've run away from a man and a woman and a cow and a horse, and now I'll run away from you!" Running even faster, he shouted,

"Run, run, as fast as you can,
You won't catch me, I'm the gingerbread man!"

The joggers ran as fast as they could after him, but there was no way they were ever going to catch him.

Then the gingerbread boy came to a river and there he had to stop. He could run but he couldn't swim.

There was a fox in the hedge who'd seen all that had gone on. He came strolling out. "Don't worry, sweet little gingerbread boy," he said. "I wouldn't dream of eating you. I've already eaten a hen and a turkey and some leftovers from a dustbin this morning. Do you want to cross the river?"

"Of course I do," the gingerbread boy said, looking over his shoulder at the man and the woman and the cow and the horse and the joggers, who were getting closer and closer.

"Then hop onto my tail," the fox said. "I'll swim you across." The gingerbread boy hopped onto the fox's tail and off they set, leaving all the gingerbread boy's pursuers behind.

When they'd gone a little way across the river, the fox said, "My tail's sinking into the water. You don't want to get wet, do you? Climb onto my back." The gingerbread boy did so.

They'd gone a little further when the fox said, "Now my body's beginning to sink too. Climb onto the tip of my nose. You'll be safer there. Gingerbread and water don't mix, do they?" The gingerbread boy climbed onto the tip of the fox's nose.

The moment the fox reached the other side of the river, he flipped the gingerbread boy up into the air and down into his mouth.

Snap! A quarter of him had gone.

Snap! A half of him had gone.

Snap! The fox ate the rest of him all in one go.

And that was the end of the gingerbread boy who'd been too fast for the man and the woman and the cow and the horse and the joggers, but not quick enough for the fox!

45

Snow White

The snow lay deep on the ground. At a window of the palace the Queen sat sewing and dreaming. As she sewed, her needle pricked her finger and three bright drops of blood fell onto her embroidery.

The Queen looked at the drops and suddenly she had a lovely thought. "If my baby is a daughter, I want her to be as white as snow, as red as blood and as black as the frame of this window," she said.

Not long after that she gave birth. Her daughter was exactly as she'd imagined her. They called the baby Snow White, but sadly her mother died within a few hours of her birth.

A year later the King remarried. The new Queen was very beautiful but so proud that she couldn't bear the thought of anyone being more beautiful than herself. In her room she had a magic mirror. She would stare into it for hours on end and ask,

> "Mirror, mirror, on the wall,
> Am I the fairest of them all?"

Without fail the mirror answered, "Yes, O Queen."

But one day, when Snow White was fourteen years old, the mirror said,

> "No, O Queen, you no longer are.
> Snow White is more beautiful by far."

The Queen was so angry and upset that she couldn't sleep or eat. What was she to do? Then she made up her mind. She sent for the royal huntsman.

"Take Snow White into the forest and kill her. Bring back her heart and liver to prove she's dead."

The huntsman led Snow White away, but when he drew his knife the girl began to cry. He couldn't kill her. "Anyway," he thought, as she ran away among the trees, "before night comes a wolf or bear will do my job for me."

A young boar came by, so the huntsman killed that instead and took its heart and liver back to the Queen. The evil woman boiled them with salt and ate them and never knew the difference.

But Snow White wasn't killed by a wolf or a bear. As night fell she came to a little house on the other side of the mountains. She knocked, but no one answered. Plucking up courage, she went inside.

Here was a sight to cheer her up – a long table with seven places set and a row of seven beds along the wall. Still no one came, and Snow White was so tired and hungry that she took a spoonful from each plate and lay down to sleep on the seventh bed.

A little later the house's owners returned. They were seven dwarfs who worked in a silver mine deep under the mountains.

"What a beautiful child!" they said, when they saw Snow White.

When she woke in the morning, Snow White was terrified by the sight of the little men, but she soon learnt how kind-hearted they were. They asked her to keep house for them, and she agreed at once.

"Take care," said the dwarfs as they set off for work. "And don't open the door. One day your stepmother will find out that you're here and again try to kill you."

And very soon the Queen did go to her mirror. Imagine her horror when it said,

> "O Queen, you are the fairest here,
>   But on the far side of the high mountains' wall,
>   In the dwarfs' neat and tidy home,
>   Snow White is still the fairest of them all."

Immediately the Queen sprang into action. Dressed as an old pedlar woman, she set off across the mountains with a tray of ribbons.

"Pretty things to buy!" she called, and knocked at the dwarfs' door. Snow White, who was looking out of the window, fell in love with the lovely ribbon the old lady held up. What harm could there be? She opened the door.

"This one, my pretty?" the Queen asked, as she fastened it round Snow White's neck and twisted and twisted. Snow White fell down as if she were dead.

And that is how the dwarfs found her that night. They cut the ribbon and slowly Snow White came back to life. It was her second escape.

Next morning the Queen went to her mirror. How angry she was when she found that Snow White was still alive. She disguised herself again and set off across the mountains.

"Pretty things to buy!" she called by the dwarfs' door. When Snow White saw the comb the old woman was holding up, she forgot all about the danger. She opened the door.

"Your hair is so beautiful, let me comb it for you," the Queen said. But the comb was poisoned, and Snow White fell down as if dead. That night the dwarfs removed the comb and brought Snow White back to life again. That was her third escape.

When the Queen went to her mirror next day, she found Snow White was still alive, and her fury knew no bounds. This time she knew that she would need her most devilish magic. She prepared an apple that was poisonous on one side only. This time she set off disguised as an old beggar woman.

"An apple for the pretty young lady?" called the Queen under Snow White's window. "It's free. No need to come to the door. I'll pass it through the window."

She saw Snow White hesitate. "Not worried it's bad, are you?" The Queen bit into the side that wasn't poisoned. "See, it's perfect." She passed the rosy apple to Snow White.

The moment Snow White bit into the poison, she fell to the ground.

The Queen peered in through the window. "Well, that's the end of you, my beauty," she said, "and good riddance." Off home she went. And next time she looked in her mirror it told her that, yes, she was the fairest of them all. How happy she was!

This time none of the dwarfs' skills could bring Snow White back to life. After three days they lost all hope, but strangely she still looked alive. Instead of burying her, they put her in a glass coffin and set it on top of a high hill.

Some time later a prince came to stay with the dwarfs. He saw Snow White in her coffin and immediately fell in love with her.

"Let me take the coffin back to my palace or I'll die," he begged the dwarfs.

The little men took pity on him, and agreed. But as the Prince's servants lifted the coffin, the piece of poisoned apple that had stuck in Snow White's throat was dislodged. She sat up, wondering where she was, and the first thing she saw was the handsome young Prince. It was love at first sight. Within a few weeks she and the Prince were engaged to be married.

One of the wedding guests was Snow White's stepmother. As soon as she entered the room, she recognized Snow White, but this time she was powerless. The servants seized her and the Prince banished her to a faraway land where she could do no more harm. From that day on, Snow White was the happiest girl in the kingdom as well as the most beautiful.

Thumbelina

Once a young wife longed and longed for a little girl of her own. Finally she got all her money together and went to a witch to ask for help.

"Is that all she gave you? That's just an ordinary barleycorn!" her husband grumbled when she got home. But the wife knew better. She planted the barleycorn and after a time it grew into a beautiful red and yellow tulip. Leaning forward, she kissed the petals softly. Very slowly and gently they opened out. And there, sitting inside the flower, was a tiny little girl. The wife loved her the moment she saw her.

Because the little girl was so small, only half as tall as a grown-up's thumb, the wife named her Thumbelina.

No one could have looked after Thumbelina better. The young wife gave her half a walnut shell for a bed, the petals of a violet for a mattress, and a rose petal for a blanket. When she wasn't sleeping, Thumbelina played on the table or listened to her mother's stories. She was very happy.

But one dark night, an old mother toad crept in through a broken windowpane and stole the little girl. "What a lovely wife she'll make you!" the toad croaked to her son, who was sitting on a lily pad in the middle of the stream. "Kark! Kark! Brek-kek-bex!" the son croaked back. He was as happy as could be at the thought of marrying Thumbelina.

But the little girl was very unhappy. "Please take me home!" she cried. One day, while the toads were away getting ready for the wedding, a shoal of minnows heard Thumbelina crying. They popped their heads out of the water. "Please help me," the little girl sobbed. The fish thought she was so beautiful that they gnawed through the root of the lily pad. It floated away down the stream.

For a week Thumbelina travelled along as happy as could be, enchanted by the wonderful sights she saw. But one day a flying beetle swooped over the water, saw how beautiful she was, and snatched her up. In great excitement, he flew to the top of a tree and called all the other beetles to come and look.

"We're going to get married!" he squeaked. "Us!"

But the other beetles, especially the ladies, didn't think much of Thumbelina at all. "Ugh! She's ugly! She's only got two legs! Where are her feelers?" they mocked. "She looks like a human!" In the end, the beetle got so tired of being laughed at for wanting to marry Thumbelina that he dropped her in a daisy.

For the rest of the summer and all of the autumn, Thumbelina lived on her own. She wove a hammock to sleep in from blades of grass and hung it under a shamrock. She took nectar from the flowers for food and drank the dew when she was thirsty. But then cold winter came. The birds flew away. The leaves fell off the trees. The shamrock shrivelled and died.

One day it began to snow. For tiny Thumbelina, each snowflake was like a shovelful of snow thrown in her face. She wrapped herself in a leaf to keep warm but it hardly made any difference. As she searched desperately for somewhere to shelter, an old fieldmouse took pity on her and called her into her nest.

"You can stay with me if you do the housework and tell me stories," the fieldmouse said. So Thumbelina was safe and happy again, until one day the fieldmouse's friend, a mole, came visiting. Then things changed. When he heard Thumbelina singing as she did the housework, the blind mole fell in love with her too.

"Come and see my house," he squeaked. "It's twenty times bigger than this."

Of course, the mole lived underground, at the end of a long, dark tunnel. He was used to never seeing the sky or the sun, but Thumbelina hated it.

"Just wait till you get there. You'll want to marry me straightaway," the mole panted, as he led Thumbelina and the fieldmouse deeper and deeper under the earth. Then Thumbelina stumbled over something on the tunnel floor.

"Never mind that," the mole called. "That died long ago." But Thumbelina stopped. She felt cold feathers. It was a dead bird. How sad! She put her ear to the bird's chest and just as the bossy mole shouted, "Hurry along! We'll be there soon!", Thumbelina felt the tiny flutter of the bird's heart.

The bird was a swallow who had hurt his wing and been left behind when the other birds flew south at the end of summer. All winter Thumbelina crept down the dark tunnel to take the swallow food and water. Slowly she nursed him back to health.

On the first day of spring, the swallow was well enough to join his friends who had flown back from the warm south. How sad Thumbelina was to see him go. The swallow had been her one true friend.

"At the end of summer," the fieldmouse said that night, "you and my friend the mole shall get married, Thumbelina. Your room is almost ready. The spiders are spinning your sheets at this very moment."

All too soon the summer had passed. On the day before the wedding, Thumbelina walked through the fields saying goodbye to the sun and the sky and all the things she'd never see again. She was quietly crying to herself when a voice above her called her name. Thumbelina looked up. It was her friend, the swallow!

"I've been thinking of you and all you did for me," he called, flying down to her. "But, Thumbelina, why are you sad?" he asked, seeing her face.

Thumbelina explained about the mole and the wedding. "Marry the mole? You don't have to do that!" the swallow cried in horror. "Climb onto my back! Come south with me and my friends. That's right – catch hold of my feathers. You're so small you won't hurt."

So, safe on the swallow's back, Thumbelina flew south. Sometimes they soared high over icy mountains, sometimes they skimmed low over plains and sandy deserts. Once they crossed a stormy sea and the spray from the waves reached up and splashed them. But all the time the air grew warmer, until one day they arrived at a place where there were many swallows' nests. Below, at the bottom of a cliff, was a field of beautiful flowers. The swallow gently put Thumbelina down on one of them.

"You'll be happy here," he said. "I know."

But Thumbelina felt sad. "Here I am again, sitting in a flower!" she thought as her friend flew away.

But what did she see before her? A young man, exactly the same size as her, was smiling at her from the nearest flower!

"You are the most beautiful girl I've ever seen," he said, and he called out to his friends. A thousand other fairies appeared among the flowers to welcome Thumbelina.

Within a month, the young man and Thumbelina were married and became the King and Queen of all the fairies. Little Thumbelina was happy at last.

56

The Princess and the Pea

Princes *must* marry princesses. There's no point in them falling in love with ordinary girls, however pretty they are. Everyone knows that, especially princes.

Once there was a prince who desperately wanted to get married. But, poor thing, he couldn't find the right princess. His mother and father the King and Queen did their best to help him. They even took their summer holidays in places where they met lots of princesses. When they got back they'd say, "Oh, by the way, we saw this lovely girl." The Prince would smile and say, "I bet she's a princess." And his parents would reply, "How did you guess? We've got her address. Why don't we invite her for a weekend?"

Unfortunately, the Prince never managed to fall in love. He *almost* fell in love. In fact, once he was engaged for over a year to a princess from Transylvania, but in the end the engagement was called off. Quite right too. They would never have lived happily ever after.

One dark November day a storm blew up. The wind lashed the palace roof so hard that tiles blew off like a storm of confetti. Trees in the royal park were uprooted, and the river burst its banks. It was so gloomy that the lights had to be put on by half past three (the King hated wasting candles), and it was so cold that the fires had to be banked right up. And the rain! It bucketed down. Not even the royal dogs, who lay sorrowfully in their baskets dreaming of sunshine and rabbits, wanted to go out.

About eight o'clock there was a knock at the palace door. A servant was sent. He came back and whispered something in the King's ear.

"Who says she's a princess?" the King asked, surprised.

"The young lady at the door says so, Sire," the servant said. "She says she lost her way. She's soaked through."

"A princess out in this weather? Whatever next?" exclaimed the King. "Oh well, I'd better come."

But the Prince was there before him. He was already on his knees before a most elegant young lady. In fact, he was on the point of asking her to marry him! Luckily the Queen arrived in the nick of time and whisked the young lady away to change her wet things.

"Well?" the King said, when the Queen came back downstairs. "Is she a princess? I bet she's just a pop star or a prime minister's daughter like all the other girls he falls in love with. I'm beginning to hate the word 'princess'. I didn't have so much trouble falling in love with a princess in *my* day." He smiled fondly at the Queen.

"I think I'll have to give her the test," the Queen said, "and hope she passes."

"Test?" queried the King. The Queen explained. "A pea? How can you tell if she's a princess with a pea?" puzzled the King.

"You just wait till morning," the Queen said, smiling.

Next morning the King paced up and down the sunlit breakfast room. "Isn't she up yet?" he asked his wife. "I hate people who lie in bed all day."

"Patience," said the Queen. "Let's see if my little plan has worked."

At last the young lady appeared. The King gasped. She looked awful, as if she'd never gone to bed at all. The Prince rushed up to her. "Darling! What's the matter?" he said. "Mother, didn't you give her our softest bed?"

"Of course I did," replied the Queen. "I put twenty mattresses one on top of the other, then twenty eiderdown quilts on top of them. What could be softer than that?"

"I feel black and blue all over," the young lady complained, as she dropped into a chair. "I'm covered with bruises the size of potatoes. That was the most uncomfortable bed I have *ever* slept in."

When he heard that, the Prince turned pale with fright. What if she left the palace and he never saw her again?

"But I did get a little sleep eventually," the young lady went on. "About four o'clock I couldn't stand it any longer, so I got out of bed and felt under the mattresses. You won't believe what I found." She held something out on the palm of her hand.

"A pea?" said the Prince. "Who left that there? I'll have their head off!"

"A pea!" said the King happily. "I understand now. Only a princess would be kept awake by a pea under her mattress!"

"Twenty mattresses," his wife reminded him.

So the Prince and Princess were married and lived a long and happy life together. And every night before they went to bed the Prince, even when he was King, checked under the mattress to make sure that no one had put even the tiniest pea there.

Little Red Riding Hood

Granny lived not far away, but to get to her cottage you had to walk through Bunny's Wood (though no one had seen a rabbit there for ages—you'll see why in a moment).

"Little Red Riding Hood!" her mother called. "Granny's still not very well. Put on your cloak and the pretty red riding hood she made for your birthday. Then pop over with this custard tart and pot of butter I've got ready for her tea."

So Little Red Riding Hood slipped on her cloak, fastened her riding hood under her chin, and set off.

"Remember to keep to the path in Bunny's Wood!" her mother called after her.

"Of course, Mummy," Little Red Riding Hood called back. "I always do."

She was only a little way inside the wood when there was a noise in the bushes and out onto the path jumped a great big wolf. Little Red Riding Hood nearly dropped her basket in fright, but actually the wolf seemed quite friendly. "Where are you off to, little girl?" he asked.

"To my granny's," Little Red Riding Hood replied. "It's the first cottage you come to at the end of Bunny's Wood. Granny's not very well. And my name's not 'little girl', it's Little Red Riding Hood."

"Sorry," said the wolf. "I didn't know. Tell you what—why don't I run ahead and tell Granny you're on your way? And, Little Red Riding Hood, don't stray off the path, will you? We don't want anything to happen to you before you get to Granny's, do we?"

Off skipped the wolf—just in time! For around the corner was a woodcutter. The wolf hadn't eaten Little Red Riding Hood there and then because he knew there was a woodcutter nearby who might come to her rescue.

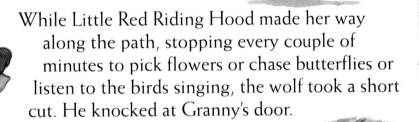

While Little Red Riding Hood made her way along the path, stopping every couple of minutes to pick flowers or chase butterflies or listen to the birds singing, the wolf took a short cut. He knocked at Granny's door.

"Who is it?" the little old lady called.

The wolf disguised his voice. "It's me, Little Red Riding Hood. I've brought some good things for tea."

"The door's on the latch, my darling," Granny called. And in went the wolf. How hungry he was! He hadn't eaten for days. He swallowed Granny whole, from her head to her feet.

About ten minutes later, Little Red Riding Hood knocked on Granny's door.

"Who is it?" the wolf called softly.

"It's me, Little Red Riding Hood."

"The door's on the latch, my darling," the wolf called. "Come on in."

For a moment Little Red Riding Hood hesitated. Wasn't there something funny about Granny's voice? Then she remembered that Granny had a cold. She lifted the latch and in she went.

The wolf was lying in bed wearing the little old lady's nightie and nightcap and glasses. The sheet was pulled right up over his face and he'd drawn the curtains to make it nice and dark.

"Put the things down there," he said, "then snuggle up to me, my darling."

Little Red Riding Hood put the custard tart and butter down on the bedside table but she didn't get onto the bed right away. Something suddenly struck her.

"What great big hairy arms you have, Granny!"

"All the better to hug you with, my darling!" the wolf said.

"And what great big ears you have, Granny!"

"All the better to hear you with, my darling!" the wolf said.

"And what great big eyes you have, Granny!"

"All the better to see you with, my darling!" the wolf said.

"And what great big teeth you have, Granny!"

"All the better to eat you with, my darling!"

With that the wolf was so excited he couldn't contain himself any longer. He threw the bedclothes aside, jumped out of bed and swallowed Little Red Riding Hood whole, head first. Then he felt so happy and full of people that he lay back and went to sleep.

Unfortunately for the wolf, he was a loud snorer. A passing huntsman heard the snores. Thinking something was wrong with Granny, he crept into the cottage. He saw at once what had happened.

"I've been looking for you for months, you wicked creature," he cried, and he hit the wolf on the head with his axe handle. Then very carefully he slit the wolf's tummy open. Out popped Little Red Riding Hood and out popped Granny! They were completely unharmed.

Granny saw the custard tart and butter she'd been brought for her tea and, well, wolfed it down. Little Red Riding Hood promised Granny that she'd never be tricked by a wolf again. As she skipped home, she noticed that the rabbits had come out of hiding and Bunny's Wood was full of bunnies again.

"What a funny afternoon it's been," she thought.

Cinderella

There was once a girl whose mother had died. When her father remarried, his new wife brought the two daughters from her first marriage to the house.

These daughters took an instant dislike to their new sister. They threw everything out of her room into the attic. Instead of treating her like a sister, they made her do all the work.

Even when she'd finished her jobs, she wasn't allowed to join the rest of the family. Instead she had to spend her evenings by the dying kitchen fire, warming her hands above the cinders – which is how she came to be called "Cinderella".

One day, however, the stepsisters received an invitation to a ball at the palace. They were thrilled. Everyone knew that the Prince wanted to get married. Perhaps he would choose one of the ladies at the ball for his wife!

The two sisters immediately set about making themselves as beautiful as possible. Unfortunately this was very difficult as, unlike Cinderella, they were rather ugly!

On the evening of the ball, when her stepsisters had driven off, Cinderella sat in the kitchen quietly crying to herself. "What's the matter, Cinderella?" a voice asked.

Cinderella sobbed, "I wish I could go to the ball myself."

"And so you shall," the voice said. Cinderella looked up, startled.

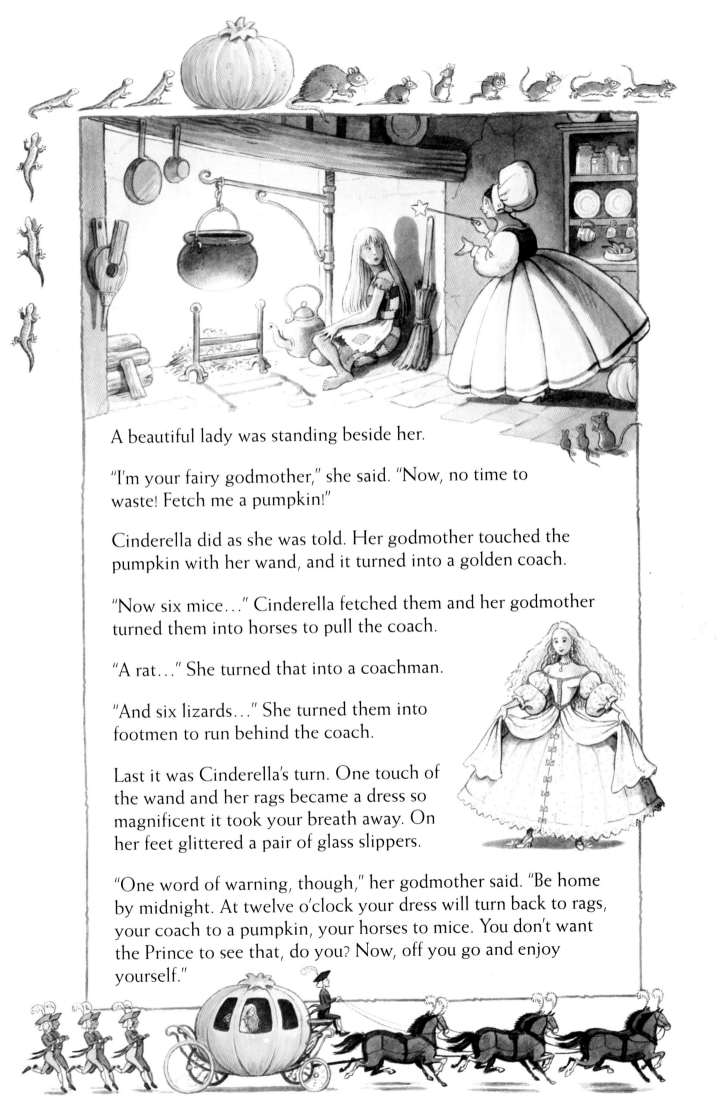

A beautiful lady was standing beside her.

"I'm your fairy godmother," she said. "Now, no time to waste! Fetch me a pumpkin!"

Cinderella did as she was told. Her godmother touched the pumpkin with her wand, and it turned into a golden coach.

"Now six mice…" Cinderella fetched them and her godmother turned them into horses to pull the coach.

"A rat…" She turned that into a coachman.

"And six lizards…" She turned them into footmen to run behind the coach.

Last it was Cinderella's turn. One touch of the wand and her rags became a dress so magnificent it took your breath away. On her feet glittered a pair of glass slippers.

"One word of warning, though," her godmother said. "Be home by midnight. At twelve o'clock your dress will turn back to rags, your coach to a pumpkin, your horses to mice. You don't want the Prince to see that, do you? Now, off you go and enjoy yourself."

That night Cinderella was the belle of the ball. The ladies (especially her two stepsisters) admired her dress and begged her for the name of her dressmaker. The gentlemen all wanted to kiss her hand and dance with her.

But the Prince fell in love with her at first sight! No one else was allowed to dance with her after that.

The minutes whirled away and it was only when the clock began to strike twelve that Cinderella remembered she should be home.

"Come back!" the Prince called, but away she ran. By the time she reached the street, her dress was rags again. All she had left was one of the glass slippers. The other was lost, she didn't know where.

That night Cinderella cried herself to sleep. She knew that life would never be so marvellous again.

But that wasn't true. The other slipper had been found on the palace steps. Next morning the Prince went round the town from house to house, begging ladies to try it on. "If I don't find the beautiful stranger who wore it last night, I'll die," he said.

At last he reached Cinderella's house. The two stepsisters tried it on. No use. It just didn't fit.

Brokenhearted, for there were only a few houses left, the Prince was about to leave when he noticed the serving-girl.

"Madam," he said gallantly, "why don't you try it too?"

"Her? Don't be silly!" the stepsisters cried.

But the Prince insisted. He'd seen how beautiful Cinderella was. And of course the shoe fitted her perfectly. Spitting with rage and jealousy, the two sisters could only look on as the Prince knelt and asked Cinderella to marry him. And she did, of course!

Jack and the Beanstalk

There was once a poor widow. Her son Jack was a lazy boy, so they had very little money. One sad day things got so bad that the widow decided to sell the only thing they had left. She sent Jack off to market with Milky White, their cow, telling him to get the best price he could.

Jack was only part way along the road when he bumped into a funny old man. The old man eyed the cow and said, "My boy, I'll swap her for something very precious." He pulled five beans out of his pocket.

"Beans?" Jack said doubtfully.

"They're magic ones," the old man explained. That made Jack's mind up. He handed over Milky White and went home very satisfied with his bargain.

"Mum! Look what I've got!" he shouted. Jack's mother wasn't so happy, though. She threw the beans out of the window and a saucepan at Jack! Then she sent him to bed without any supper.

In the morning, however, Jack could hardly believe his eyes. Something was growing outside his bedroom window. He poked his head out. It wasn't a tree or a giant sunflower but a beanstalk that grew straight up into the sky. At once Jack clambered out of his window and began to climb the beanstalk.

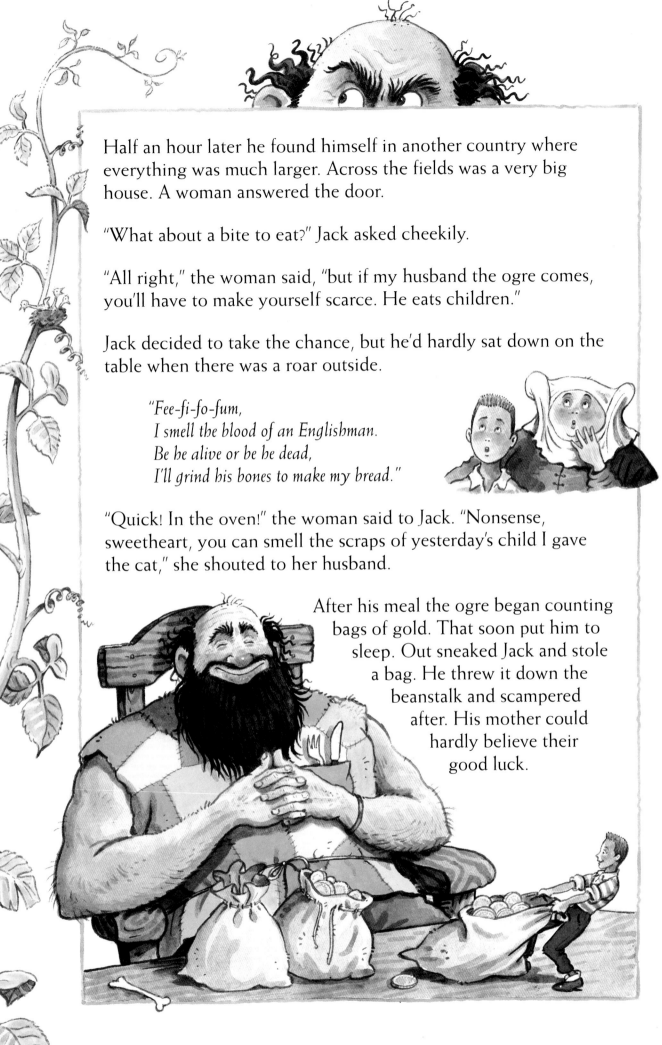

Half an hour later he found himself in another country where everything was much larger. Across the fields was a very big house. A woman answered the door.

"What about a bite to eat?" Jack asked cheekily.

"All right," the woman said, "but if my husband the ogre comes, you'll have to make yourself scarce. He eats children."

Jack decided to take the chance, but he'd hardly sat down on the table when there was a roar outside.

"Fee-fi-fo-fum,
I smell the blood of an Englishman.
Be he alive or be he dead,
I'll grind his bones to make my bread."

"Quick! In the oven!" the woman said to Jack. "Nonsense, sweetheart, you can smell the scraps of yesterday's child I gave the cat," she shouted to her husband.

After his meal the ogre began counting bags of gold. That soon put him to sleep. Out sneaked Jack and stole a bag. He threw it down the beanstalk and scampered after. His mother could hardly believe their good luck.

But a few months later, all the gold spent, Jack decided to go back to the other land. Up the beanstalk he climbed. This time, however, the ogre's wife was more suspicious.

"Last time you came, a bag of gold went missing," she complained. "The fuss that caused!" All the same she let Jack in.

Very soon the ogre came along. *"Fee-fi-fo-fum,"* he started to roar. Jack hid in the oven again.

"Nonsense, angel," the ogre's wife said. "It's only the smell of that baby broth you had yesterday. Eat your buffalo pie."

After he'd eaten, the ogre shouted, "Wife, bring me my hen." His wife brought it. "Lay!" the ogre commanded, and to Jack's amazement the hen laid a golden egg. Naturally Jack stole the hen too.

By now Jack and his mother were well off, but after a year Jack decided to try his luck again. Up he climbed. This time he sneaked his way past the ogre's wife and hid in her copper pan.

In came the ogre. *"Fee-fi-fo-fum,"* he started.

"If it's that dratted boy again, he'll be in the oven, dearest," his wife said.

But of course Jack wasn't.

"I know he's here somewhere," the ogre rumbled, but although they searched high and low they couldn't find him.

This time after his meal the ogre got out a golden harp. "Sing!" he commanded, and the harp lullabyed him to sleep. Now Jack wanted that harp more than anything he'd ever wanted before. He climbed onto the snoring giant's knee, jumped onto the table and grabbed it.

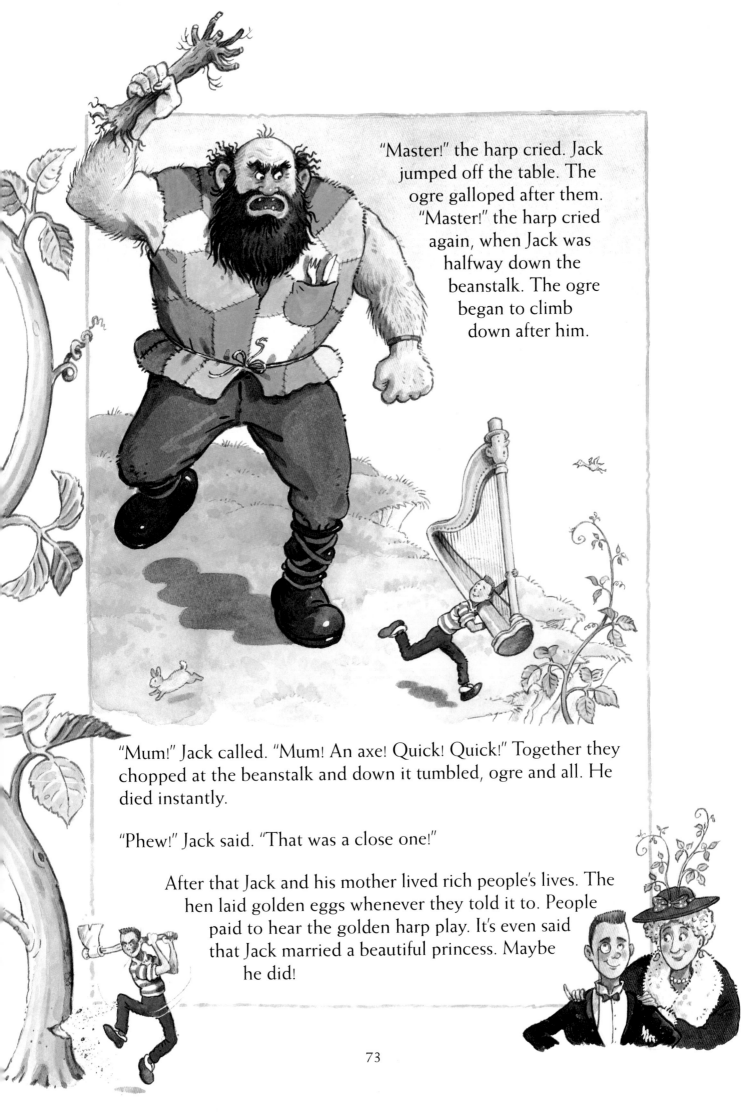

"Master!" the harp cried. Jack jumped off the table. The ogre galloped after them. "Master!" the harp cried again, when Jack was halfway down the beanstalk. The ogre began to climb down after him.

"Mum!" Jack called. "Mum! An axe! Quick! Quick!" Together they chopped at the beanstalk and down it tumbled, ogre and all. He died instantly.

"Phew!" Jack said. "That was a close one!"

After that Jack and his mother lived rich people's lives. The hen laid golden eggs whenever they told it to. People paid to hear the golden harp play. It's even said that Jack married a beautiful princess. Maybe he did!

Beauty and the Beast

Once there was a rich merchant who had three daughters. Two of them were totally selfish, but the third, Beauty, was kind and loving.

One day the merchant received news that his ships had sunk in a great storm. He had lost all his money and was left with nothing but a tiny cottage in the country. The two greedy sisters hated it. They refused to do anything except lie in bed and moan. All the work was left to Beauty.

After a time, however, the merchant heard that one of his missing ships had reached port. Before he set off to claim it, he asked his daughters what presents they'd like him to bring back. The greedy sisters cheered up straightaway.

"Dresses and jewels!" they begged.

"And you, Beauty?" the merchant asked.

"A rose. That will be enough for me," Beauty said.

A few days later, the merchant sadly began his ride home. He was as poor as ever, for he had been cheated out of his money. As he entered a forest, the night drew in. It was dark and cold. A blizzard blew and the snow piled into drifts. Wolves howled in the distance.

For hours the merchant and his horse stumbled about, lost, until suddenly, straight ahead, a bright light shone from a magnificent castle. But this was the strangest of castles, for although there were fires in the grates and lights burnt in every room, no one was about. The merchant called and called. No one came. Eventually he tethered his tired horse in the stables and sat down at the castle's high table to eat the meal laid out there. Then he went to bed.

In the morning, he found new clothes laid out for him. Downstairs a cup of steaming hot chocolate had been put out for his breakfast.

"This castle must belong to a good fairy who has taken pity on me," the merchant said. "If only I could thank her."

As he was leaving, the merchant passed a bed of roses. "At least I can keep my promise to Beauty," he thought. He snapped off a stem of blossoms. Immediately there was a bellow of rage. From behind the bushes leapt a terrible beast, so ugly that the merchant almost fainted.

"You ungrateful man!" the Beast roared. "I saved your life! I fed and clothed you! Now you steal my beautiful roses. You must die at once!"

The merchant fell to his knees. "That rose was for one of my daughters, my lord," he said.

"I am no lord, I am a Beast," the creature snarled. He towered over the merchant. "And as for your precious daughters, go and see if one of them will save your life by coming to live with me. If not, in three months you will die."

The merchant rode home sorrowfully through the sunlit forest. At home the two sisters paid hardly any attention to the story of his terrible adventure. They were infuriated that he'd brought them no dresses or jewels. But Beauty was different.

"Father, let me go," she begged.

"You deserve to," the sisters said. "If it hadn't been for your stupid rose, the Beast wouldn't have wanted to kill our father."

Three months later the merchant returned to the castle with Beauty. All was as before: the empty castle, the meal ready on the table. Then, when they'd finished eating, the Beast appeared. Beauty trembled, for he was as dreadful as her father had described, or worse!

"Have you come here of your own free will?" the Beast demanded.

"Yes," Beauty replied.

"In that case your father must leave in the morning and never set foot here again."

So next morning Beauty was left alone. At first she cried, but then she remembered a dream she'd had. In it a lady had told her, "Beauty, your bravery in saving your father will be rewarded."

Beauty cheered up. Perhaps after all things might go well. She walked through the gardens, looking sadly at the rose beds, then explored inside the castle. Imagine her surprise when she found a door with her name on it. Inside, the room was exactly as she'd have furnished it herself, full of books and musical instruments.

"The Beast cannot mean to harm me," she thought, "if he intends me to enjoy myself so much."

Beauty took out a book. On it was written in letters of gold, "Here you are Queen. Your wish is my command."

"If only I could see what my father is doing now!" she cried out loud. And she could – in the mirror on the far side of the room. As the picture faded, Beauty felt less lonely and homesick.

That night at supper, the Beast appeared. "Beauty," he asked timidly, "may I watch you?"

"You are master here," Beauty said.

"No," the Beast replied. "You are the mistress. I will go if you wish." The Beast hesitated. "But tell me, do you find me unbearably ugly?"

Beauty didn't know what to say, then looked him straight in the face. "Beast, I have to tell the truth. I'm afraid I do."

When she had finished her meal, the Beast had one more question. "Beauty," he asked, "will you marry me?"

"No, Beast, never."

The sigh the Beast gave echoed round the castle.

Every night at nine o'clock, the Beast came to talk. Beauty found she liked him more and more. She even fretted if he was late. If only he wasn't so ugly! If only he wouldn't keep asking her to marry him! She dreaded having to refuse and hearing the haunting sigh he gave afterwards.

"You may not love me, Beauty," he said, "but you'll never leave me, will you? Promise that." For three months it went on like this.

Then one day Beauty saw in the mirror that her father was ill. At once she asked the Beast if she could go home to nurse him.

"Beauty, you must go," the Beast replied. "You know that I will die of grief if you don't come back, don't you? I am afraid that you will stay at your father's, but if you want to come back, just put your ring on your bedside table. The next morning you will wake in my castle."

"I will return in a week," Beauty promised.

Next morning Beauty woke in her own warm bed in her father's cottage. How overjoyed he was to see her! It made him better at once. That afternoon her sisters, who had both got married in the meantime, came round to visit. How jealous and angry they were when they saw that their father's favourite had come back.

"Listen!" one said to the other. "Let's trick her. Let's persuade her to stay a second week. Then the Beast will come and kill her." Instead of moaning and criticizing her, the two sisters rubbed onions in their eyes and pretended to cry at the thought of Beauty leaving. Beauty promised to stay another week.

Yet soon Beauty found that she was missing the Beast as much as she'd missed her father. As she slept she had a terrible dream, in which the Beast was lying cold and lifeless on the castle lawn. She sat bolt upright in bed. How could she have been so heartless? Quickly she pulled off her ring and put it on the bedside table. When she woke again, she was in the Beast's castle.

That evening she waited for him. Nine o'clock struck. He didn't come. Quarter past struck too. Suddenly full of dread, she ran through the castle and out into the gardens. The Beast lay on the lawn. She had killed him! Forgetting his appearance, Beauty threw herself upon him. His heart was still beating!

"I thought you would never come back. I tried to starve myself to death," he whispered.

"But I love you, Beast!" Beauty said. "I want to marry you."

Then something amazing happened. The castle seemed to become even more beautiful, more full of light. Beauty gazed around, then turned back to the Beast. But the Beast had gone. In his place a handsome young prince lay on the lawn.

"I want the Beast," Beauty cried. The Prince stood up.

"I *am* the Beast," he said. "An evil fairy put a spell on me. She turned me into something unbearably ugly. I would have stayed like that for the rest of my life, if you had not said you would marry me."

The Prince led Beauty into the castle. There she found her father and the lady she'd seen in her dream, the good fairy.

"Beauty," the good fairy said, "you have got your reward."

She waved her wand. In an instant everyone in the hall was transported to the Prince's kingdom, where the Prince's subjects greeted him with cheers and applause. Soon Beauty and her Beast were married. They became the happiest Prince and Princess that ever lived.

Goldilocks and the Three Bears

Once upon a time three bears lived in a house in the woods. They were called Tiny Little Bear, Middle-sized Bear and Great Big Bear. Their house, which they kept very spick and span, was full of just the right-sized things – bowls, cups, spoons, chairs, beds – anything you could think of.

One morning it was Great Big Bear's turn to get breakfast. He ladled the porridge into the bowls, just the right amount in each. But when they sat down to eat, the porridge was far too hot. The three bears decided to go for a walk while it cooled.

Two minutes after they had set off, who should come past their house but a little girl called Goldilocks. Goldilocks was a naughty spoiled brat who always did exactly what she wanted. She shouldn't even have been in the woods (her mummy had sent her to the shop to buy some milk). But there she was and she knew the bears were out walking. She tried the door. It wasn't locked, so in she went.

Goldilocks spied what was on the table. "Porridge!" She licked her lips. "My favourite!" She tried the porridge in Great Big Bear's bowl first. "Ugh!" she said. "That's far too hot." She spat it out.

Next she tried Middle-sized Bear's bowl. "Ugh! That's far too cold!" She spat that out too.

Last she tried Tiny Little Bear's. "Goody!" she said. "That's just right!" She gobbled it up. "Bother!" she said. (Actually she said a far worse word.) "There wasn't much in there."

Then, because she needed a rest after all her wandering about in the woods, Goldilocks tried Great Big Bear's chair. "Hard as rocks," she said. "No good to me."

Next she sat in Middle-sized Bear's. "Miles too soft," she said.

Last she tried Tiny Little Bear's chair. "Just right," she said. At least she thought it was until her bottom went through the seat and the chair collapsed! Again she used a very bad word.

But Goldilocks was determined to get a rest. Upstairs she went and opened the bedroom door. First she tried Great Big Bear's bed, but that left her head too much in the air.

Next she tried Middle-sized Bear's. That left her feet too far up.

Last she tried Tiny Little Bear's. It was perfect! Without even taking off her shoes, she tucked herself in and went straight to sleep, dreaming of all the naughty things she'd get up to when she was older.

Meanwhile the bears returned home. They hung their coats up neatly and went to eat their porridge. Except, except…

"Who's been at my porridge?" Great Big Bear growled. "They've even left the spoon in it."

"And who's been at mine," asked Middle-sized Bear, "and done the same?"

"And who's been at mine, and eaten it all up?" Tiny Little Bear sobbed.

The three bears looked about. Someone had been in their house without permission and they didn't like that one bit.

"Somebody's been sitting in my chair," Great Big Bear growled, "and tossed my cushion on the floor!"

"Somebody's been sitting in my chair too," growled Middle-sized Bear. "My cushion's squashed."

"And somebody's been sitting in my chair and broken it," Tiny Little Bear said. He began to cry again.

"Sshh!" Great Big Bear said. "What's that noise?" The three bears listened.

"It's someone snoring," said Middle-sized Bear. The three bears looked at each other.

"They're still here!" Tiny Little Bear said. Upstairs they crept.

They went into the bedroom. "Somebody's been lying on my bed," Great Big Bear growled. "My cover's all creased."

"Somebody's been lying on my bed too," Middle-sized Bear grumbled. "The pillow's all out of place."

"And somebody's been lying *in* my bed, and they're *still* lying in it," squeaked Tiny Little Bear.

Great Big Bear's voice hadn't woken Goldilocks—she'd thought it was the wind roaring in her dream. Middle-sized Bear's voice hadn't woken her either—she'd thought it was her teacher shouting and that didn't frighten her at all. But Tiny Little Bear's shrill voice woke her straightaway.

She took one look at the bears standing in a row along one side of the bed, jumped out the other side and dived through the window. She landed in a bed of flowers only planted last week, knocked over the bird-table and ran straight out of the garden.

"She hasn't shut the gate," Middle-sized Bear complained with a sigh. "One of us will have to do it."

And what happened to Goldilocks no one knows. Maybe her mother just scolded her for not bringing the milk. Or maybe she did something worse, when she found out what Goldilocks had *really* been up to!

The Ugly Duckling

Deep in the bushes a duck was sitting on her eggs. She was bored with being on her own, so when the eggs began to crack she jumped off the nest with a quack of pleasure.

"Now I can get back to the farmyard," she thought, "and show off my new family!" She counted her cheeping ducklings to make sure they were all there. Oh no! One egg hadn't hatched.

"That's a large one left in your nest," another duck who was passing said. "I bet it's a turkey's."

"A turkey's egg? No, it's mine," the mother duck said crossly. With a sigh she settled back on top of it.

When the last duckling hatched, it was very large and ugly. To tell the truth the mother duck was rather ashamed of it.

All the same, her other ducklings were as pretty as could be and she didn't want to stay away from the farmyard another minute. She led her little family straight out onto the water.

"At least the ugly one swims very well," she said to herself. "So it can't be a turkey. Turkeys can't swim, can they? Perhaps it will get prettier as it grows older. Perhaps it will stop being so big."

Unfortunately the opposite happened. The ugly duckling grew bigger every day and all the other ducks noticed how different he was. Hardly a minute passed without him being attacked and bitten and jeered at. Even his brothers and sisters quacked, "We wish the cat would get you!" The chickens bullied him and the girl who fed them kicked him out of the way.

Finally the ugly duckling couldn't bear it any longer. He flew over the fence and scuttled away until he came to the place where the wild ducks lived. But the wild ducks thought he was ugly too and would have nothing to do with him.

So the duckling became the loneliest creature in the world. Even the little birds from the trees and hedges flew away when he came near. "It's because I'm so ugly," he said to himself.

He wandered here and there, always on his own. Once he made good friends with two young wild geese, but they flew away to escape the hunters. Once an old lady took him into her house, but her pets, a hen and a tom cat, laughed at the strange bird for liking the water and not being able to lay eggs. So the ugly duckling ran away again.

The leaves turned yellow and brown. Snow-laden clouds hung over the land. One evening at sunset, a flock of tall, handsome birds with dazzling white feathers came out of the bushes in front of the duckling. They had long, elegant necks that swayed backwards and forwards.

"Wait!" called the duckling, but the birds spread their enormous wings and were soon high in the sky. The duckling couldn't help himself. He turned round and round in the water like a spinning top and dived to the bottom in sheer excitement. From his throat came a strange loud cry, so strange it frightened him. He couldn't forget those white-feathered birds. Whatever they were, he loved them.

It was a long, hard winter. Several times the ugly duckling nearly died. Once he became frozen in the ice and a passing farmer had to rescue him. But at last spring came and the duckling found that he could fly properly, not just flip-flapping above the water but soaring high in the sky.

One day he was testing his new-found strength when, below in a river, he saw more of the beautiful white birds. He did not hesitate. "I'll fly down," he thought. "Even if I'm ugly, I want to be near them." And he landed on the water.

Two children were throwing bread to the white birds from the river bank. When they saw the duckling, they called to their mother, "Look! A new swan! He's even more beautiful than the others!"

At first the duckling didn't realize what they meant. Instead he bowed his head in shame as the tall white birds turned to look at him. "Kill me!" he thought. "I don't care what you do."

Then, as he raised his head, he caught sight of his own reflection in the water. And he couldn't believe what he saw. His neck was long. He had beautiful white feathers.

"Welcome!" the other swans called. They glided towards him; not angry with him or full of hate like the birds in the farmyard, but bowing their necks gracefully towards him as if to say, "You're beautiful!"

"A swan!" he said in wonder. "I'm not an ugly duckling at all. I'm a swan!"

The Elves and the Shoemaker

There was once a shoemaker who was very poor although he was a master craftsman. Every day he seemed to get even poorer. In the end he sold so few shoes that he had no money to buy leather to make new ones. At last he only had one piece of leather left.

That night he cut out the leather and, with a sigh, left it on his workbench ready to stitch up into his last pair of shoes in the morning. As he went upstairs to bed, he could only think that if a miracle didn't happen he would have to sell his shop.

The next morning, when he opened his workroom door, the shoemaker saw something extraordinary. On his bench stood the most beautifully made pair of shoes he'd ever seen. He darted to pick them up. He turned them round in his hands. He couldn't have made them better himself!

That morning a rich man walked past the shop. He saw the pair of shoes in the window and liked them so much that he was willing to pay twice what the shoemaker asked!

Now the shoemaker had enough money to buy leather for two more pairs of shoes. That evening he cut them out and left them on his workbench. In the morning, to his great joy, the leather had been stitched up into *two* beautiful pairs of shoes. The shoemaker was able to sell them for enough money to buy leather for *four* pairs of shoes.

For some time, things went on like this. Soon the shoemaker's little shop became so famous that rich ladies and gentlemen from all over the country came to see what he had to sell.

But one day towards Christmas, the shoemaker, who was a kind-hearted man, said to his wife, "Don't you think we ought to see who's doing us this favour? Think how poor we once were and how well off we are now. Tonight let's stay downstairs with the light off and see who comes." So instead of going to bed, the shoemaker and his wife hid behind the workroom door. As quiet as mice they waited.

As midnight struck from the tower of the parish church, the shoemaker's wife nudged her husband. Two tiny elves, dressed in rags, were clambering up onto the workbench. They ran around looking at what work they had to do. Then they seized the shoemaker's tools and began. As they worked they sang,

"Stitch the, stitch the, stitch the shoes,
  Fit for kings and queens to choose!
  Dart the needle, pull the stitch.
  Work, work, work, to make the cobbler rich!"

Long before dawn they'd finished their work and slipped away.

The shoemaker and his wife got up late next morning. Over breakfast the wife said, "Think how cold those poor little creatures must have been! Their feet were bare and their clothes were just rags. It made me shiver just to look at them. Don't you think we ought to make them a present to say 'thank you' for all the work they've done for us?"

The shoemaker agreed, and he and his wife set to work immediately. That night they left the tiniest clothes and shoes you could imagine on the workbench.

At midnight, as the church clock struck, the elves appeared again. At first they seemed puzzled to find no shoes to stitch, but suddenly they realized what kind of presents had been left for them. With whoops of joy they pulled on the tiny clothes and shoes. Then they began to dance all around the room, leaping on and off the table, balancing along the backs of the chairs, and swinging off the curtains. As they played they sang,

"The shoemaker has no more need of elves.
Now let him stock his own shelves!"

With that they ran out of the door and across the churchyard. They never came back. The shoemaker was sad to see them go but he could hardly complain after all the work they'd done for him. And they seemed to leave a little of their magic behind them, for he and his wife were lucky for the rest of their lives.